This book belongs to

. . . .

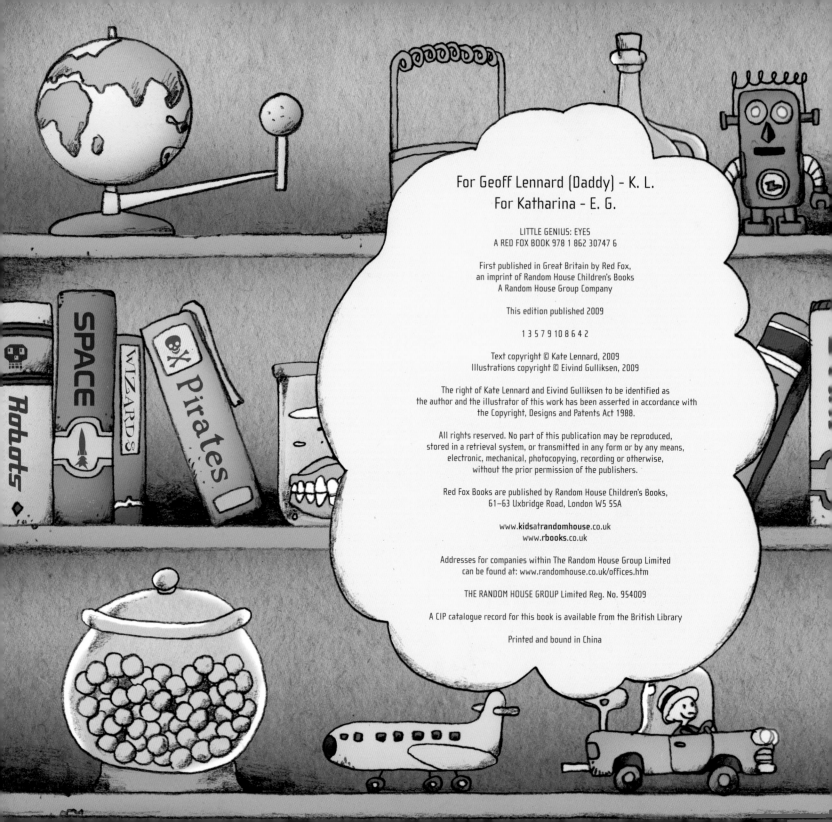

For Geoff Lennard (Daddy) – K. L.

For Katharina – E. G.

LITTLE GENIUS: EYES
A RED FOX BOOK 978 1 862 30747 6

First published in Great Britain by Red Fox,
an imprint of Random House Children's Books
A Random House Group Company

This edition published 2009

1 3 5 7 9 10 8 6 4 2

Red Fox Books are published by Random House Children's Books,
61–63 Uxbridge Road, London W5 5SA

www.kidsatrandomhouse.co.uk
www.rbooks.co.uk

Addresses for companies within The Random House Group Limited
can be found at: www.randomhouse.co.uk/offices.htm

THE RANDOM HOUSE GROUP Limited Reg. No. 954009

A CIP catalogue record for this book is available from the British Library

Printed and bound in China

Hello!
I'm **Little Genius**.

I've been looking into the human body and all the interesting bits that make it work.

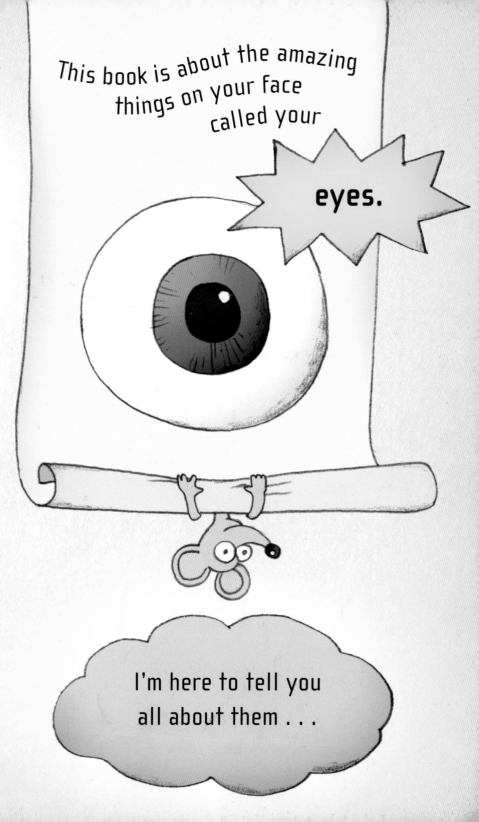

This book is about the amazing things on your face called your **eyes.**

I'm here to tell you all about them . . .

Did you know that your eyes are actually ball-shaped? That's why they get called **eyeballs**.

Eyes go on the front of the head because it's a good place to look out from. Anywhere else wouldn't get such a great view!

This is what your head bone looks like with no skin or hair on.

Eyeballs sit in the holes here.

Can you feel the bones around your eyes?

If you could touch an eyeball it would feel squashy.
Like a grape!

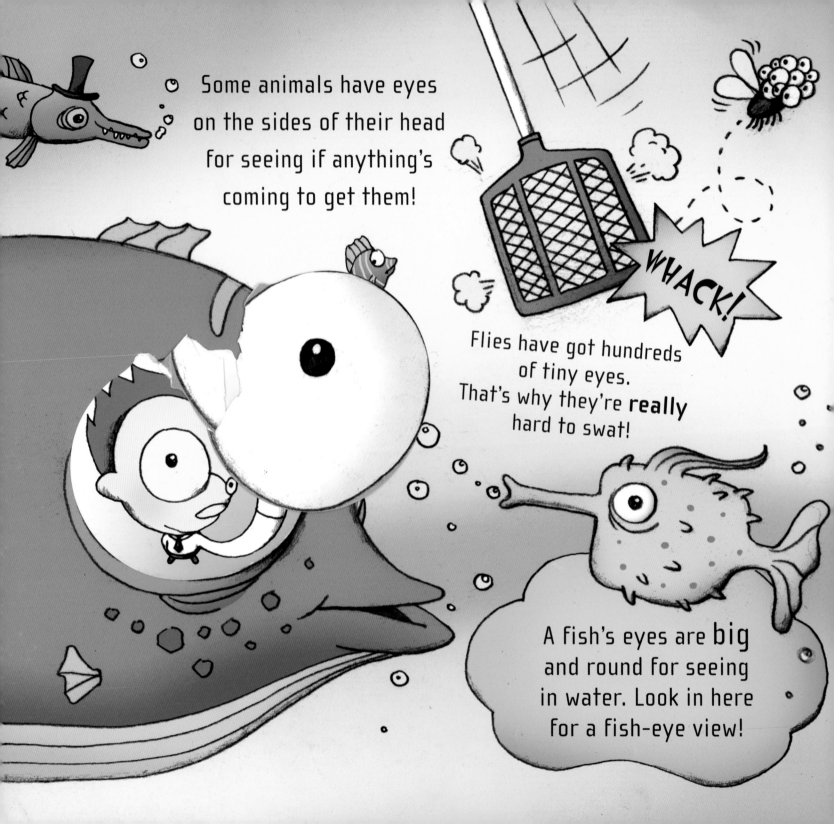

Let's have a really good look at an **eye**.

The coloured bit is called the **iris**. You can get blue, brown, green or a mixture. What colour eyes have you got?

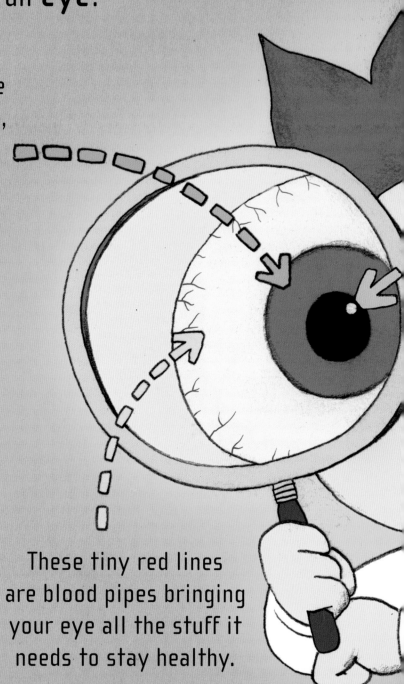

You are_
Little Genius

Computers can tell who someone is just by looking at their iris!

These tiny red lines are blood pipes bringing your eye all the stuff it needs to stay healthy.

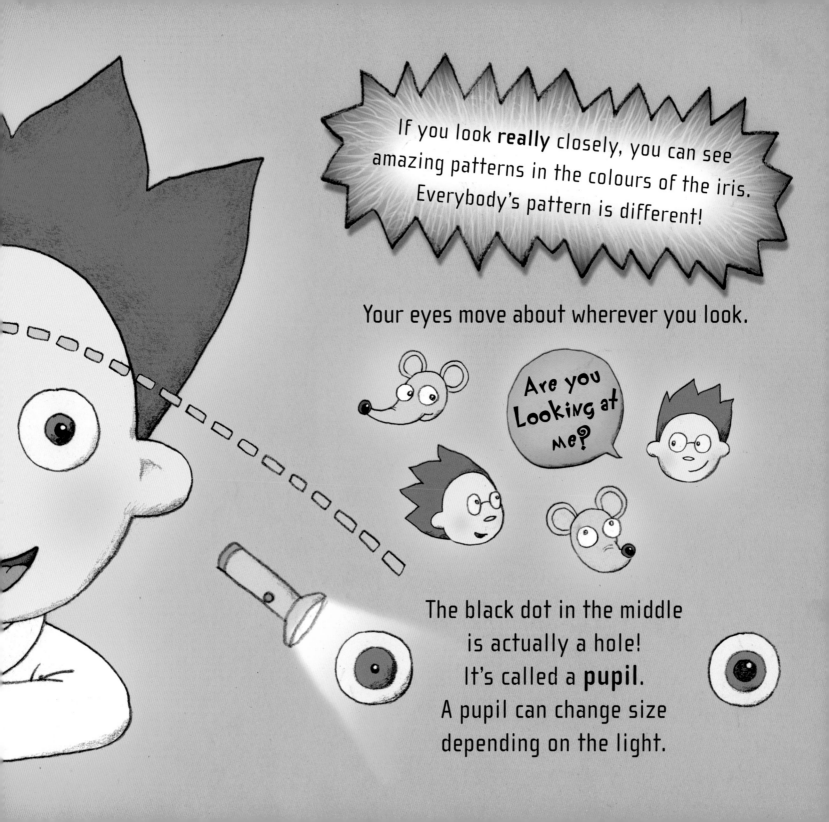

This is what you'd see
if you cut an eye in half.
This is just a model –
don't ever do it in real life!

This isn't just an empty
space. It's full of clear **goo**
to keep the eye healthy
and squashy.

This bit is called
the **lens**. It's like
a see-through
stretchy plate.

The orange
line is called
the **retina**.

Can you see the clear
bump over this bit?
It's called the **cornea**.

goo

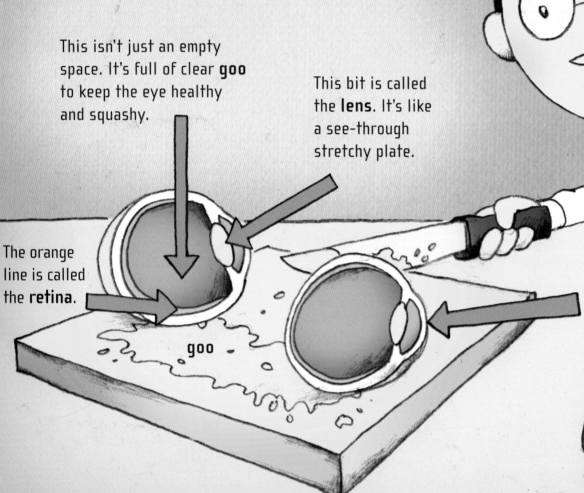

The white is only on the outside, like the peel of an orange.

So how do **eyes** work?

Eyes are like your body's windows. If you don't have them, you can't see out!

When I pull
up this blind
I'm letting in
the light.

That's exactly what your eyes do when they open.
They let in the light!

Everything you see starts off as **light.**

Have you ever looked behind you when you've been to see a movie? The light shines out from the back, over the rows of seats, and lands at the front as pictures on the screen.

The back of your eye is a bit like a movie screen!

The picture goes in upside down!

retina

pupil

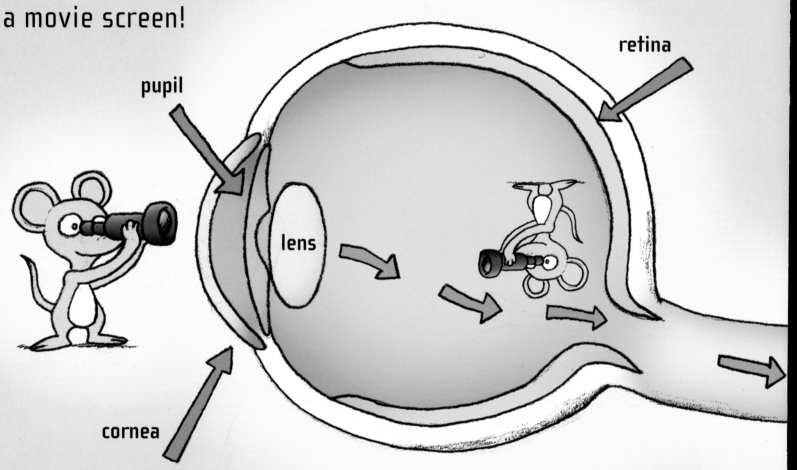

lens

cornea

The picture hits the cornea and is flung down the pupil to the lens, through the goo and onto the retina.

The messages get sent up these wires at the back to a big computer called your brain.

Your brain flips it over for you when it gets there. If it didn't, we'd think everything was on the ceiling!

Your **brain** can understand the messages and tells you what you are seeing.

Cats' eyes are bigger than ours. They have larger pupils which let more light into their eyes.

Have you ever noticed the lights in the road at night? They're called 'Catseyes' because the man who invented them copied how a cat's eye works.

He got the idea when a real cat's eyes stopped him driving into a wall!

Like a mirror, eyes don't work properly if they're dirty.

Eyelids are a bit like windscreen wipers on a car!

Every time you blink, your **eyelids** come down and give your eyes a wipe.

Eyelashes and **eyebrows** help to keep out dust, too.

Eyes have got a brilliant cleaning mixture called tears. They are made of salty water.

If your eye really hurts or you're upset about something, tears can overflow. They dribble down your cheeks and your nose pipes.

That's why you get a runny nose!

Sleeping is really good for your eyes. It gives them a good wash and a soak.

To keep your eyes healthy and safe, don't:

Read in the dark.

Look straight at the sun.

Use other people's eye drops.

Wear other people's glasses.

Some people have a problem seeing clearly.

An eye doctor will do an **eye test** to find out
if you need glasses.

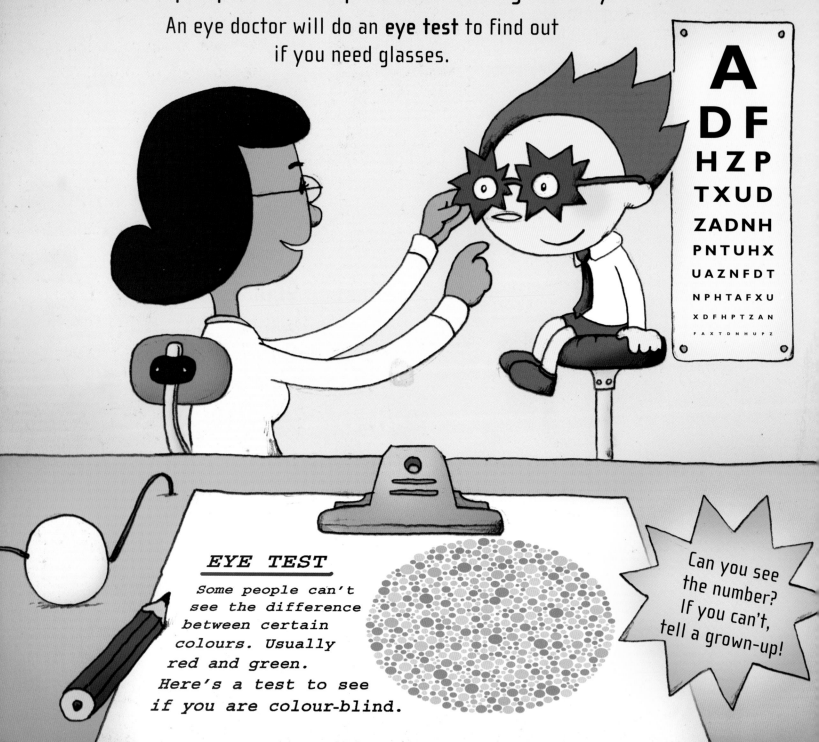

A
D F
H Z P
T X U D
Z A D N H
P N T U H X
U A Z N F D T
N P H T A F X U
X D F H P T Z A N
F A X T D N H U P Z

EYE TEST

*Some people can't
see the difference
between certain
colours. Usually
red and green.
Here's a test to see
if you are colour-blind.*

Can you see
the number?
If you can't,
tell a grown-up!

Some people are blind. This means their eyes don't work. They can have special dogs to help them.

Glasses are fun to choose!

They have lenses to fix any fuzziness.

CooL!

Sometimes children get a lazy eye. They have to wear an eye patch over the good one so the lazy one can catch up.

Healthy eyes can do brilliant tricks!
Like these:

Is this a duck or a rabbit?

Look at all the dots, are they black or white?

Stare at this fish and count to 30 slowly.

Is this book open or closed?

Now look at the fish bowl.
Can you see it go in? What colour is it?

That's everything I found out about eyes.

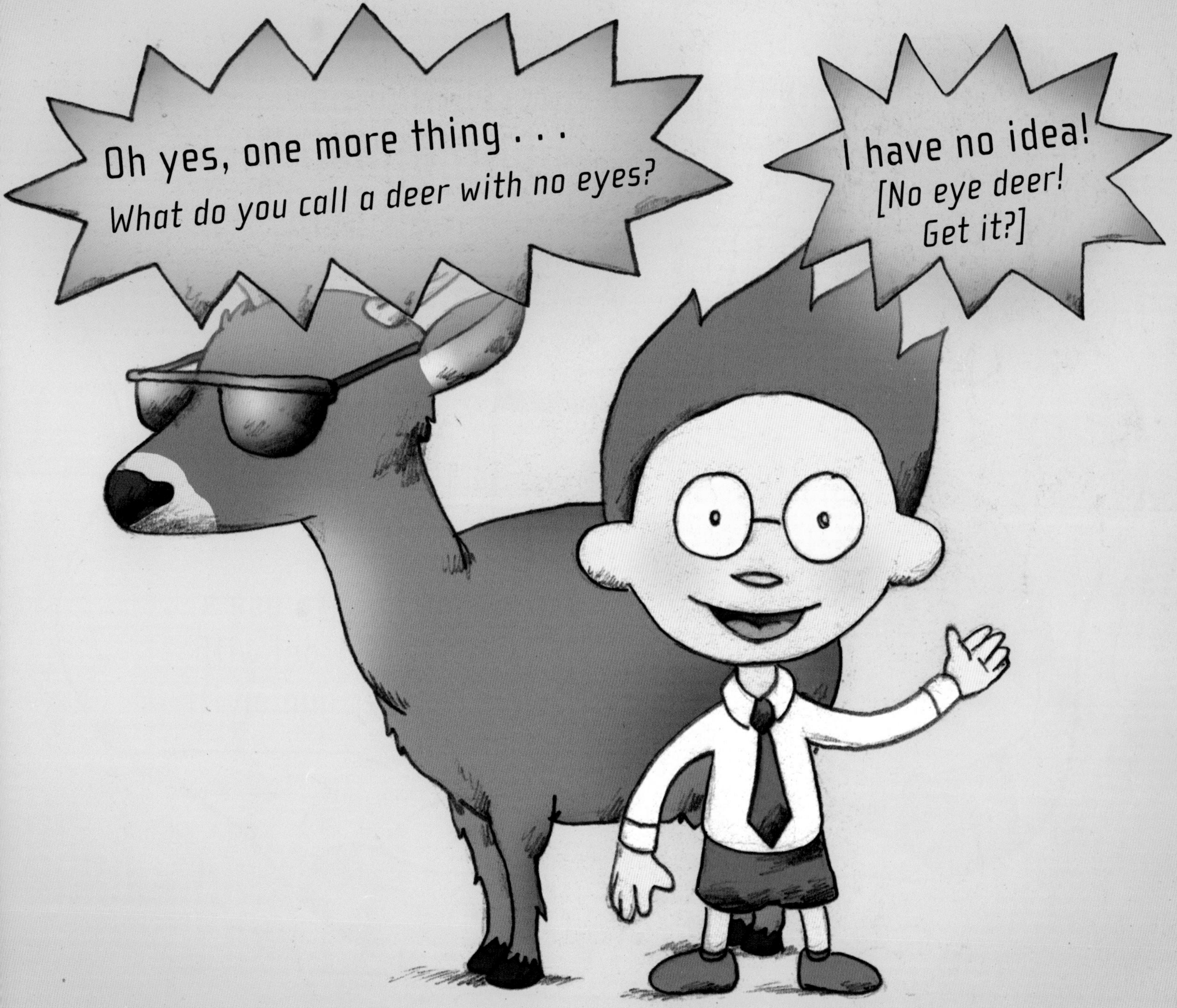

I'd quite like to be an ophthalmologist when I grow up.

Would you?

More **Little Genius** books
for you to enjoy

DIGESTION

9781862307452

BONES

9780099451631

BRAINS

9780099451624

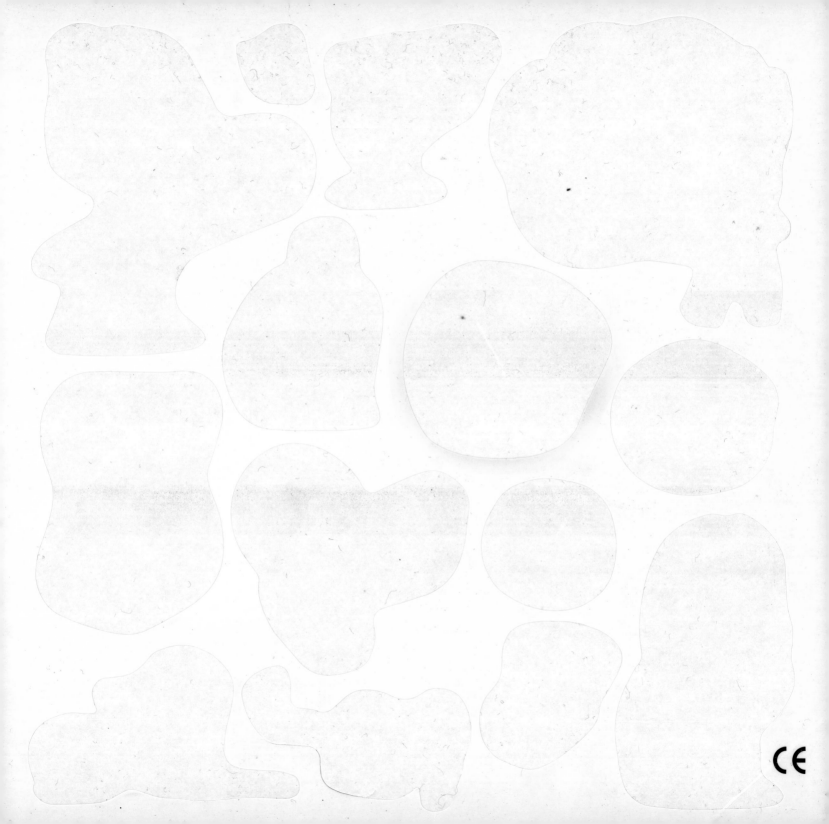

CE